LAND OF THE EMU PEOPLE

BY PERCY TREZISE

Angus&Robertson
An imprint of HarperCollins*Publishers*

This saga, JOURNEY OF THE GREAT LAKE, is dedicated to my colleague of many years, Aboriginal author and artist Dick Roughsey. It is also dedicated to all my Aboriginal friends who led me through their temples of Dreamtime, passing on the legends and stories of their race memory, which records their history back through countless millennia, recalling the dramatic humid and arid weather phases of the Ice Age.

The saga is set circa 30,000 years ago to encompass the extinct megafauna of marsupials, reptiles and birds, the giants of Dreamtime, which shared this ancient land with the people of those times.

Percy Trezise

Angus&Robertson
An imprint of HarperCollins*Publishers*, Australia

First published in Australia in 1998
This paperback edition first published in 2002
by HarperCollins*Publishers* Pty Limited
ABN 36 009 913 517
A member of the HarperCollins*Publishers* (Australia) Pty Limited Group
http://www.harpercollins.com.au

HarperCollins*Publishers*
25 Ryde Road, Pymble, Sydney, NSW 2073, Australia
31 View Road, Glenfield, Auckland 10, New Zealand
77-85 Fulham Palace Road, London W6 8JB, United Kingdom
Hazelton Lanes, 55 Avenue Road, Suite 2900, Toronto, Ontario M5R 3L2
and 1995 Markham Road, Scarborough, Ontario M1B 5M8, Canada
10 East 53rd Street, New York NY 10022, USA

National Library of Australia Cataloguing-in-Publication data:

Trezise, Percy.
Land of the Emu people.
ISBN 0 207 19634 6. (hbk.)
ISBN 0 207 19882 9. (pbk.)
1. Aborigines, Australian - Legends - Juvenile literature.
I. Title. (Series : Journey of the Great Lake ; 4).
398.20994

Printed in Hong Kong through Phoenix Offset on 128gsm Matt Art

9 8 7 6 5 4 3 2 1   02 03 04 05

INTRODUCTION

Aboriginal oral history tells of hundreds of Dream Roads criss-crossing
the Australian continent which were made by Ancestral Beings during their travels
at the beginning of Dreamtime. It also tells of a vast freshwater lake
at the top of Australia and stories about ancestors like the Anta Moola sisters.

There is also scientific evidence to suggest that 36,000 years ago there was a large
freshwater lake at the top of Australia. Scientists called it the Lake of Carpentaria . . .
and it was also known as Balanorga, the big water.

This is the story of three children and their journey around Balanorga,
along the Dream Road of the Anta Moola sisters, to find their way home.

Percy Trezise
Cairns, Queensland
1998

Jadianta, Lande and Jalmor survived a trip across the vast lake Balanorga during a great storm. To find their way home they have travelled through the land of the Dingo People and the land of the Magpie Goose People, facing fierce crocodiles and giant goannas. They are in new and unfamiliar land.

Goobala and his wife Labamor had been fishing upstream when they saw Jadianta's smoke signal. They decided to camp with the Kadimakara children because it was nearly dark and at night the crocodiles in the river were dangerous.

The next morning they all paddled across the river and Goobala pointed out the pathway of the Anta Moola sisters leading south, saying that if they followed it for two days they would find some Emu People in a lakeside camp. Lande and her dingo, Lasca, led the way followed by Jadianta and little Jalmor. They lit fires so that the Emu People would know they were coming.

Two nights later the children of the Kadimakara People arrived at the Emu camp. It was joking time around the cooking fires and the happy people welcomed the Kadimakara children having seen their morning smoke signals and showed them to a vacant *gunyah*.

While they were eating Jadianta told the Emu People of their adventures since the great storm. Later young dancers painted their bodies and mimed the storm-tossed voyage, the crocodile attack and the battle of the giant goannas.

The land of the Emu People was close to the land of the Snake People, the Punga-lungas, who were very dangerous. The Emu People urged the three young wayfarers to stay a few days with them before continuing their long journey home. The Emu language was similar to Dingo and other languages of the western shore that the children had learned, and the children found it easy to understand. Lande and Jadianta decided Jalmor should have a few days rest and time to play with the Emu children.

Lande joined a group of girls and women to gather waterlily bulbs and seeds while Jadianta and other boys went with the men who were going to burn grass to keep green shoots growing for the animals. They would also spear wallabies flushed out by the fire.

The grasslands were burnt in patches, fires being set only where there was old dry grass under the new grass. Burning patches every few days provided a constant supply of green grass well into the dry season and made hunting easy as the men knew where the grazing animals would be feeding.

The larger animals, kangaroos, emus and kadimakara, didn't mind the fires burning near them, but the tall grass was the smaller wallabies' cover and the fires forced them to flee into the open where eager spearmen waited.

The fire-stick party was nearing camp carrying their wallabies when they heard a distant wailing. It came from a group of women running toward the camp from the other side. Something dreadful had happened.

The women said a raiding party of Punga-lunga men had sneaked up on them at the lily lagoon and carried off three girls. The women had fought the raiders with their digging sticks but were clubbed down by the big Punga-lunga men. One of the missing girls was Lande.

Jadianta was stunned and horrified as was little Jalmor who wailed and cried. Jadianta tried to comfort his younger brother. He said, 'We will get her back from the terrible Punga-lungas. We will not go home without Lande, we must find her somehow.'

A party of young Emu warriors had gathered together and set off at a run for the lily lagoon to pick up the tracks. The raiders must be caught before they reach the safety of their own country, the land of the Snake People. The Emu warriors had dingoes with them to continue tracking at night.

In the middle of the next day the Emu People were disappointed to see the warrior band returning empty handed. The Punga-lungas had beaten them to the boundary river and crossed to safety among their numerous warriors.

The Emu People told Jadianta that the Punga-lungas, or Snake Men, had always beaten them in battles. Only now they had a secret weapon. The Woomera People, whose country lay on the far side of the Snake People, had invented a spear-thrower which enabled a spear to be hurled three times further than a hand-thrown spear, however the Emu People did not want to attack. They did not want to reveal their secret weapon yet.

Jadianta met Doogul and Marnie, brothers of the two girls captured with Lande. Jadianta said, 'The Emu warriors cannot invade Snake country, so we must rescue our sisters on our own. We must find out where the girls are being held.'

Jadianta called Lasca and held Lande's headband out for her to smell. He placed it around her neck and said, 'Go to Lande, find Lande.' Lasca gave him a steady stare. Gently pushing her southward, he kept saying, 'Lande, find Lande.' The little dingo trotted south — she understood her mission.

T wo days later Jadianta was awakened
at dawn by Lasca licking his face.
The headband was gone from her neck,
instead she wore Lande's wallaby-tooth
necklace. Lasca had found Lande and
would be able to lead them to her.
Jalmor cried and hugged the little dingo.

The Emu boys, Doogul and Marnie, said
they should travel at night because the
Punga-lungas were terrified of evil spirits
they called Mulgans which roamed after
dark. The moon cycle was just ending and
there would be no moon for the next two
nights. It was the perfect time to go.

Jadianta, Doogul, Marnie and Lasca walked all day until they reached the river on the boundary of Snake country. Shallow water on a rocky bar provided a crossing safe from crocodiles and the three boys and their dingo hid among reeds to await nightfall, eating food from their dillybags.

When it was dark Lasca led the way. Jadianta saw that the dingo was following the Dream Road of the Anta Moola sisters. They would have to travel this way again.

All night they walked, circling out at times to pass groups of flickering campfires. Just on dawn they reached the lake shore and the growing light of the rising sun revealed a small island nearby with many *gunyahs* — Lande's prison.

The island was only a spear-throw away and the boys hid in some reeds to watch old women paddling *walpas* over and back. They realised that the captive girls were going to be held there until they were old enough to marry. The old women were guards and as no *walpas* were left on the island at night, the girls could not escape.

The boys waited till dark then untied a *walpa* each and paddled across. Lasca leapt ashore and vanished among the *gunyahs*. In a short while the waiting boys saw four shadowy figures approaching with Lasca. They were their three sisters with a younger girl.

Lande hugged Jadianta then helped her new friend, a young girl, Wongabel, of the Woomera clan, and Lasca on to the *walpa*. The girls had all stolen paddles for the rescue they hoped would come and together they paddled swiftly to shore. On reaching Snake land they fell into single file, trotting after the little dingo as she led the way north.

The sun was much higher as they neared the shallow crossing and it was then they heard the sounds of pursuit. The alarm had been sounded on the island and a large party of Punga-lunga warriors were racing for the crossing. They were close behind as Jadianta and the others ran through the shallow water.

Jadianta splashed along after the girls and Lasca. He was worried — he knew they could not run fast enough and the fastest Punga-lungas would catch them before they reached the other side. The Punga-lungas would kill the three boys and recapture the girls. All was lost. Then his heart leapt with new hope — spears were flying overhead. It was the Emu People!

When the Emu People realised the three boys had gone to rescue their sisters, they sent a large party of Emu warriors to set up an ambush at the crossing. They hurled woomera-flung spears from behind bushes to keep their new weapon secret and now the Punga-lungas were falling everywhere.

The Punga-lungas fell back in disarray dragging their dead and wounded with them and howling in fury as they saw the party of boys and girls disappear into the bushes.

Jadianta was overjoyed to have Lande back. He thanked Doogul and Marnie and the Emu warriors for their help, but now he realised that the Punga-lunga People of the Snake and Kangaroo clans were a fearful barrier they had yet to cross on their long journey home.

Jadianta, Lande and Jalmor continue to travel along the Dream Road of the Anta Moola sisters
and in the *Land of the Snake People* they meet their strongest adversaries so far.
They will have to cross many boundaries; travel through the *Land of the Snake People*
and face the ferocious Kangaroo People on their long journey ahead.
Will they ever see their family again?

GLOSSARY

Ancestral Beings   people who came down from the stars at Creation Time and turned
    into every species of life on earth; animal and plant
Anta Moola sisters   two Ancestral Beings who travelled around Balanorga during Dreamtime
Balanorga   the name for the great lake; bala=big, norga=water
Dingo People   a clan on the west side of the creek
Dream Road   the path of an Ancestral Being during Dreamtime
gunyah   a shelter
kadimakara   a bullock-sized marsupial similar to a wombat
Kadimakara People   a clan on the east side of the lake
mulgans   a Snake word for evil spirits
Punga-lungas   both Snake and Kangaroo People with deep-set eyes and sloping foreheads
walpas   rafts
woomeras   a sling used to throw spears